THIS BLOOMSBURY BOOK
BELONGS TO

....

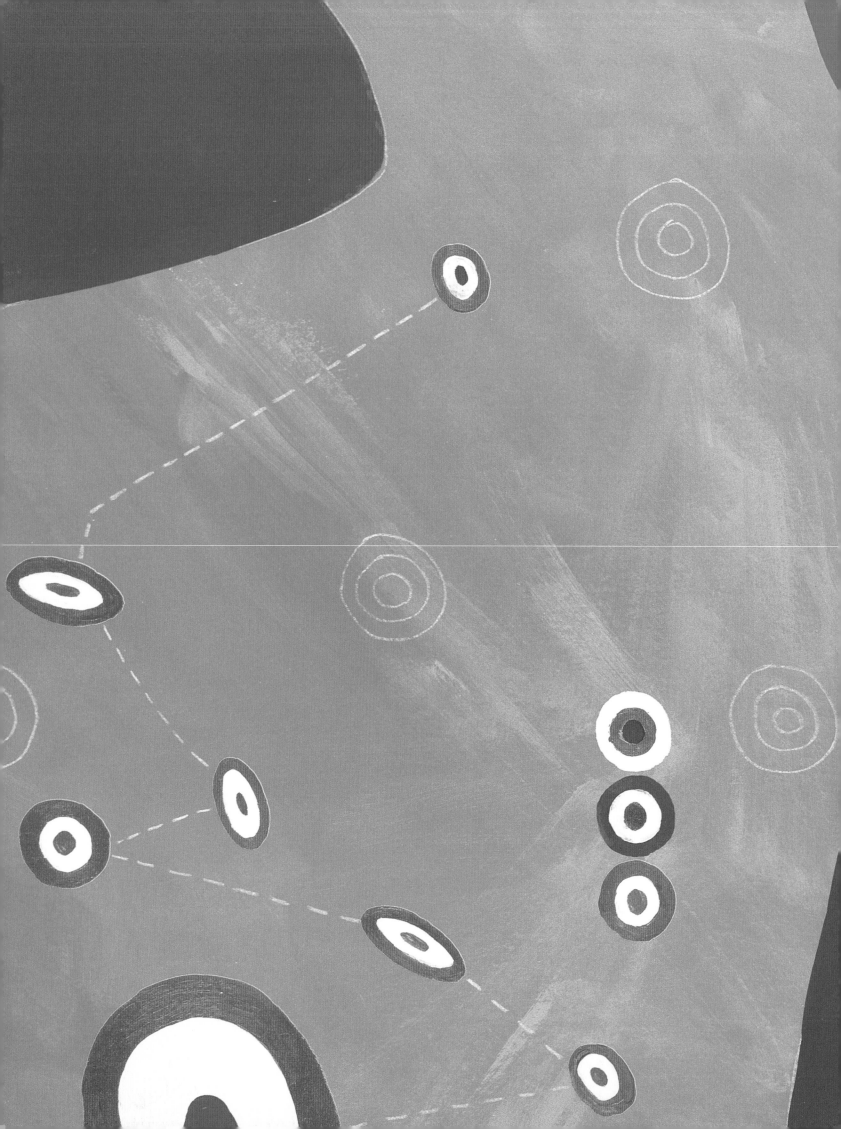

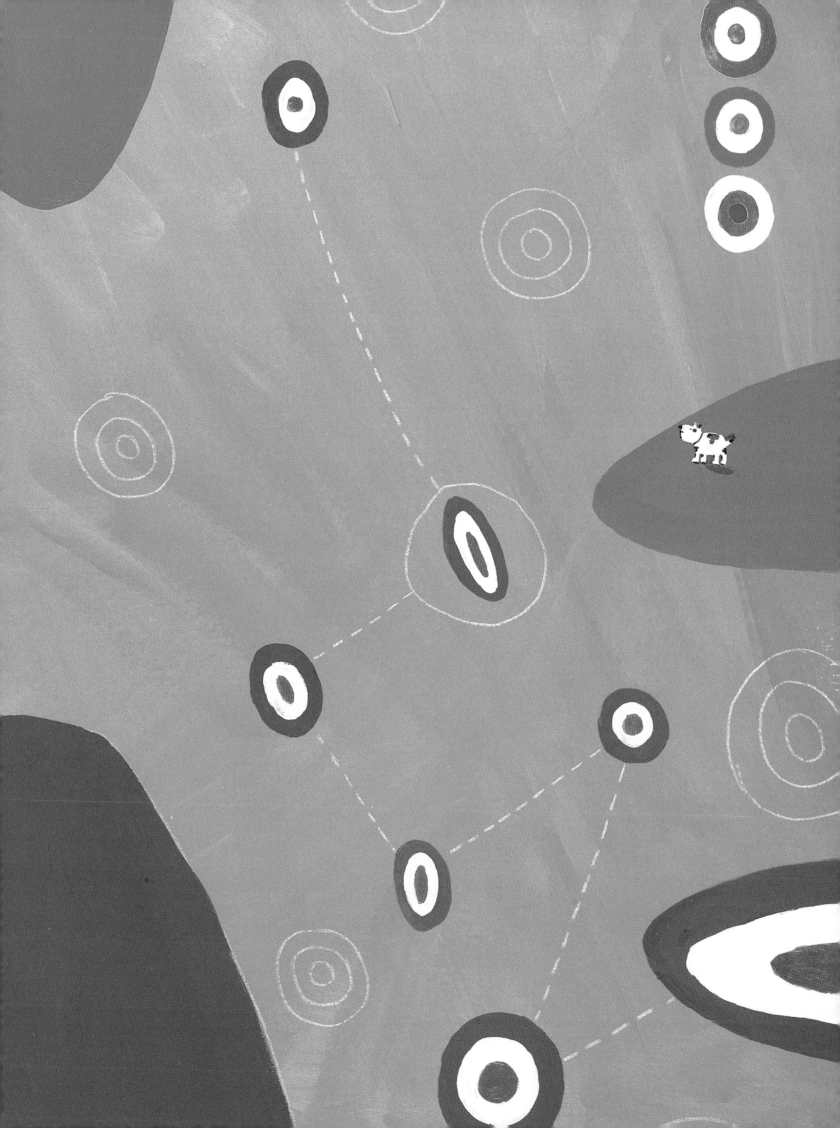

To the real Patrick, of course! – KL
For Gran – AJ

First published in Great Britain in 1998 by Bloomsbury Publishing Plc
36 Soho Square, London, W1D 3QY

This revised paperback edition first published in 2008

A CIP catalogue record of this book is available from the British Library

ISBN 978 0 7475 9775 9

Designed by Dawn Apperley

Printed and bound in Belgium by Proost

1 3 5 7 9 10 8 6 4 2

All papers used by Bloomsbury Publishing Plc are natural, recyclable products made from wood grown in well-managed forests.
The manufacturing processes conform to the environmental regulations of the country of origin

www.bloomsbury.com/childrens

WHAT!

Kate Lum and Adrian Johnson

BLOOMSBURY
CHILDREN'S
BOOKS

Once there was a boy named Patrick, who went to visit his Granny for the night. As it was getting dark, Granny said to Patrick,

'Oh Patrick! It's getting dark, get into bed now dear, and go to sleep.'
'But Granny . . .' said Patrick,

'I don't HAVE a bed.'

'I don't HAVE a bed.'

'WHAT!!!?'
cried Granny. She ran to the yard,
where some fine trees were growing,
and chopped one of them down.

She got her hammer and her nails
and made Patrick a bed.

Then she painted it a lovely shade of blue,
brought it into the house and put a bright,
red mattress on it.

'There you are dear,' said Granny.
'Now get into bed, put your head on the
pillow, and go to sleep.'

'But Granny,' said Patrick,
'I don't HAVE a pillow.'

'WHAT!!??' cried Granny.
She ran to the hen house, where some chickens
were sleeping, and got a load of feathers.

She found a piece of cloth and made a bag and
stuffed the feathers into it and sewed it up and
put it on the bed.

'There you are, Patrick,' said Granny.
'A nice comfy pillow. Now lie down, put your
head on the pillow, pull up your blanket, and
go to sleep.'

'But Granny,' said Patrick,
'I don't HAVE a blanket.'

'WHHAAT!!??'

cried Granny. She ran outside to
where some fat sheep were snoozing, and
sheared off some of their wool.

She combed it and spun it and made it into yarn, and knitted the warmest blanket she could. Then she dyed it a lovely shade of purple, and when it was dry she spread it on the bed.

'Now Patrick,' said Granny, 'lie down on your bed,
put your head on the pillow, pull up your blanket,
and go to sleep. And don't forget your teddy bear.'

'But Granny,' said Patrick,
'I don't HAVE a teddy bear!'

'WHAAAT!!??' cried Granny.

She ran into the living room. She took down the curtains, cut them into the shape of a bear, stuffed them full of cotton, sewed on some button eyes, tied on a red ribbon, and gave this bear to Patrick.

'Now Patrick,' said Granny.

'GO to your bed.

LIE down upon it.

PUT your head on the pillow.

PULL up the blanket.

CUDDLE with your teddy bear.

And

GO TO SLEEP!'

'But Granny . . .' said Patrick.

'It's already morning.'

'WHAAAT!!!???'
cried Granny.

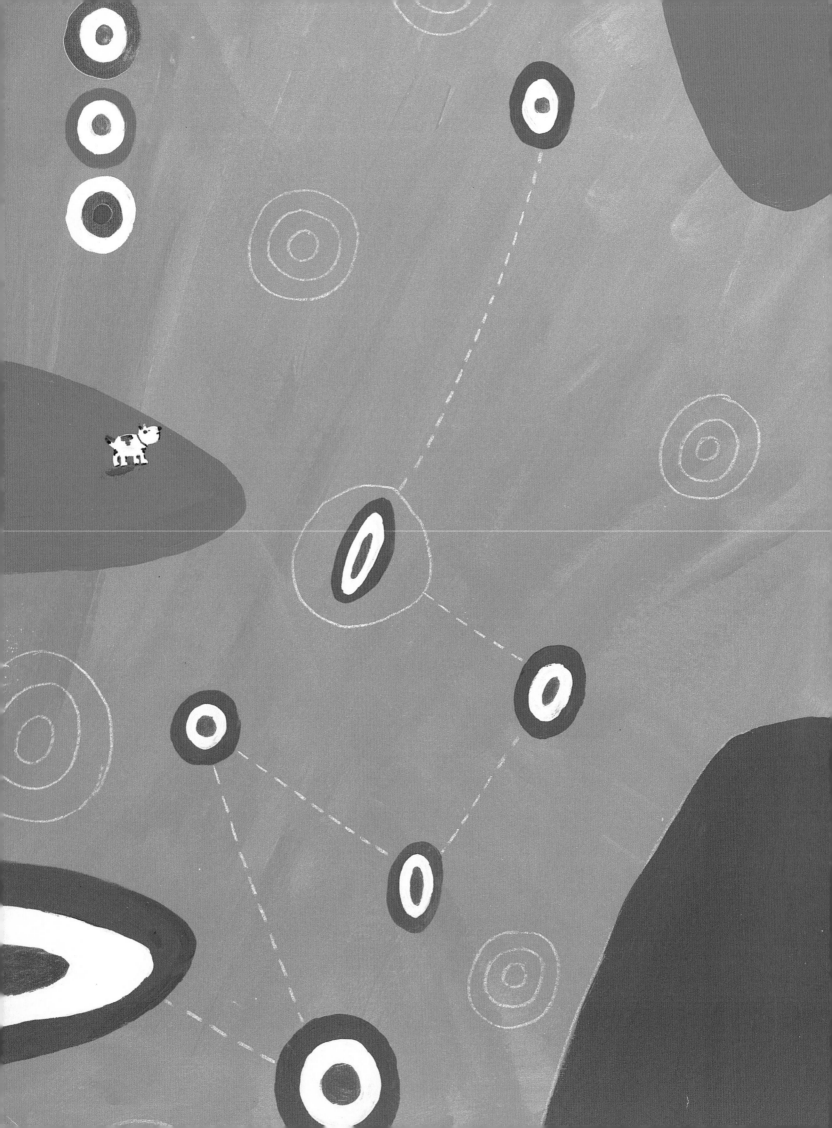

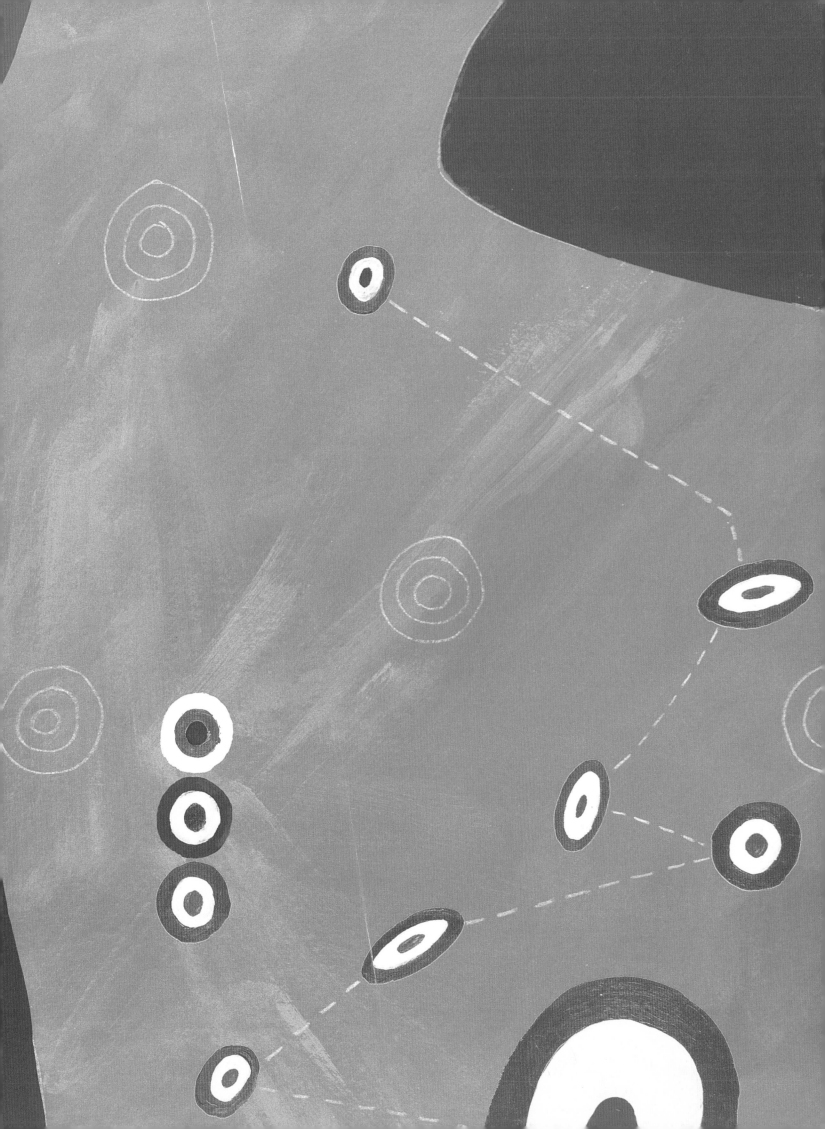

Acclaim for this book:

'The repetition is perfect and had us all in stitches'
The Times

'Great use of colour'
Glasgow Herald

'A quirky cautionary tale'
Bookseller

'Kate Lum's fantastical accumulating story has a great ending, and Adrian Johnson's pictures repay the most detailed inspection'
Guardian

'There are many books that hope to coax a child to sleep. *What!* by Kate Lum and Adrian Johnson, is a deliciously exaggerated example of the genre'
Observer